Harleigh's Hospital Heads To Hawaii

Written by Karen Arnold   Illustrations By Anastasia Ward

Peaches Publishing

Illustrations copyright 2024 Anastasia Ward Illustrations
All rights reserved.
anastasiawardillustrations.com

Hardcover: 979-8-8691-1883-7
Paperback: 979-8-8757-1016-2

First paperback edition January 2023

Edited By Jena Benton | JenaBenton.com
Layout By Anastasia Ward | AnastasiaWardIllustrations.com

Published By Peaches Publishing

DEDICATION

To the resilient inhabitants of Lahaina, Hawaii,
who have risen from the ashes
after enduring unimaginable heartbreak.
May time help you heal and keep the spirit of
Aloha alive in your hearts.

Harleigh finally had a moment to herself when news of a Hawaiian hurricane interrupted her program.

"Hey everyone! Listen to this!" shouted Harleigh above the hustle and bustle of her hospital.

She turned up her TV and her friends heard the horrible news.

Many animals had been harmed and many had lost their homes.

Hamster and Hedgehog
came to a halt.

Hector the Hippo
stopped eating his hamburger.

Helen the Horse worried about her cousin, Horace
who lived in a hut on a Hawaiian beach.

"We must go help our
Hawaiian friends and family!"
announced Harleigh.

And without hesitation,
her friends hastily began loading
hospital supplies into a helicopter.

"Ready when you are, Harleigh!"
hollered Henry the Hyena.

"Hey! Wait for me!" shouted Hector.

"Hang on!" warned Henry.

"We're a little heavy!"

Everyone huddled together and hoped for the best.
They held on tight with no land in sight.

"There he is!" exclaimed Helen.

It was a harrowing sight as her friends heroically rescued Horace, who was hanging onto a palm tree.

"I can't believe you came here for me, Helen," said Horace, humbly.
"I was beginning to lose hope. Thank you from the bottom of my heart."

Once everyone was safely on the ground, they couldn't help but shout, "Hooray!"

However, once the howling winds had died down, the animals emerged from hiding. Some of them had headaches. Some of them needed homes. And some of them simply needed a hug or a hand to hold.

Helen and Horace started rebuilding the hut.

Hamster and Hedgehog were busy handing out bandages.

Harleigh and her other friends certainly had their hands full as they worked day and night

in hopes of healing those who were hurt.

As the sun rose the next morning, Harleigh realized she had fallen asleep. She looked around and noticed the animals were healing nicely, but something was wrong.

None of them looked happy.

"How can this be?" Harleigh thought to herself.

Hector walked over to Harleigh and asked her what she was thinking about.

"I don't understand why everyone looks so unhappy," she said.

"Maybe they're just feeling a little heartbroken," offered Hector.

"Yes. A hurricane is a hard thing to overcome," sighed Horace who had overheard their conversation.

Harleigh saw the hurt in Horace's eyes.

"I know how to heal their bodies," she said, "but how do I heal their broken hearts?"

Horace thought for a moment.

"How about a luau?!" he announced excitedly.

"What's a luau?" asked Hector.

"It's a Hawaiian feast with dancing!"
answered Horace.

"That sounds heavenly," said Harleigh,
"but I'm hopelessly exhausted."

"I've got this!" Hector exclaimed.
"I'm great at hospitality!"

And with help from Hamster and Hedgehog,
he hurried off to plan the best luau the island animals
had ever seen!

As the sun set on the horizon and the animals were enjoying their feast and hula dancing, Harleigh looked around. She was proud of their hard work.

"When are we going home?" asked Hector.

"Home is where your heart is,"
replied Harleigh happily
as she reached for Horace's hand.

"And home is with your Ohana,"
added Horace.

"What's Ohana?" asked Hector.

"Ohana means family,"
answered Helen as she gave Horace a great big hug.

Horace's heart was full.
For not only did he have family...

...they were here.

Made in the USA
Monee, IL
23 December 2024

72487169R00019